TITLES IN SERIES I AND III OF THE
MINI CLASSICS INCLUDE:

SERIES III

Alice Through the Looking-Glass
Brer Rabbit's Riding Horse (and other Stories)
Brer Rabbit and the Turtle Race (and other Stories)
The Cat that Walked by Himself
The Elephant's Child (and How the Camel got his Hump)
The Fox without a Tail (and other Aesop's Fables)
The Golden Goose
Hush-a-Bye Baby (A Collection of Prayers
    and Lullabies)
The Little Match-Girl (and The Swineherd)
A Little Princess
Peter and the Wolf
Peter Pan
The Pied Piper of Hamelin
The Princess and the Pea (and The Red Shoes)
The Remarkable Rocket
Rumpelstiltskin
The Sorcerer's Apprentice
Tom Thumb
Wind in the Willows III – The Adventures of Toad
Wind in the Willows IV – Return to Toad Hall

This edition printed for:
Shooting Star Press, Inc.
230 Fifth Avenue–Suite 1212,
New York, NY 10001

Shooting Star Press books are available at special
discounts for bulk purchases for sales promotions,
premiums, fund-raising, or educational use. Special
editions or book excerpts can also be created to
specification. For details contact: Special Sales
Director, Shooting Star Press, Inc., 230 Fifth Avenue,
Suite 1212, New York, New York 10001.

ISBN 1-56924-245-3

Printed and bound in Great Britain.

The Mole had been working very hard all the morning, spring-cleaning his little home. First with brooms, then with dusters; then on ladders and steps and chairs, with a brush and a brimming pail; till he had dust in his throat, small splashes of white-wash all over his black fur, and an aching back and weary arms. Spring was moving in the air above and in the earth below, entering even his dark and lowly little house with its spirit of change.

It was small wonder, then, that he suddenly flung down his brush on the floor, said, "Bother!" and "O blow!" and also "Hang spring-cleaning!" and bolted out of the house without even waiting to put on his coat.

Something far off was calling him imperiously, and he made for the steep little tunnel which led to the fresh air far above. So he scraped and scratched and scrabbled and scrooged, and scrooged again. He scratched and scraped, working busily with his little paws and muttering to himself, "Up we go! Up we go!" till at last, pop! his snout came out into the sunlight, and he found himself rolling in the warm grass of a great meadow.

"This is fine!" he said to himself. "This is better than whitewashing!" The sunshine struck hot on his fur, soft breezes caressed his heated brow, and after the long seclusion of his underground home, the singing of happy birds fell on his dulled hearing almost like a shout. Jumping off all his four legs at once, in the joy of living and the delight of spring without its cleaning, he pursued his way across the meadow till he reached the hedge on the further side.

"Hold up!" said an elderly rabbit at the gap. "Sixpence for the privilege of passing by the private road!" He was bowled over in an instant by the impatient and contemptuous Mole, who trotted along the side of the hedge chaffing the other rabbits as they peeped hurriedly from their holes to see what the row was about. "On___

Onio___

Then they all started grumbling crossly at each other. "How stupid you are! Why didn't you tell him—" "Well, why didn't you say—" "You might have reminded him—" and so on, in the usual way; but of course, it was then much too late, as is always the case.

med too good to be

hrough

thrusting — everything happy, and progressive, and occupied. And instead of having an uneasy conscience pricking him and whispering "Whitewash!" he somehow could only feel how jolly it was to be the only idle dog among all these busy citizens. After all, the best part of a holiday is perhaps not so much to be resting yourself, as to see all the other fellows busy working.

And so, over hill and down dale, he meandered aimlessly along.

He thought his happiness was complete when he suddenly came to the edge of a full-fed river. Never in his life had he seen a river before — this sleek, sinuous-bodied animal, chasing and chuckling, gripping things with a gurgle and leaving them with a laugh, to fling itself on fresh play-mates that shook themselves free, and were caught and held again. All was a-shake and a-shiver — glints and gleams and sparkles, rustle and swirl, chatter and bubble.

The Mole was bewitched, entranced, fascinated. By the side of the river he trotted as one trots, when very small, by the side of a man, who holds one spellbound by exciting stories; and when tired at last, he sat on the bank, while the river still chattered to him, a babbling procession of the best stories in the world, sent from the heart of the earth to be told at last to the insatiable sea.

As he sat on the grass and looked across the river, a dark

hole in the bank opposite, just above the water's edge, caught his eye, and dreamily he fell to considering what a nice snug dwelling-place it would make for an animal with few wants and fond of a bijou riverside residence, above floor-level and remote from noise and dust. As he gazed, something bright and small seemed to twinkle down in the heart of it, vanished, then twinkled once more like a tiny star — but it could hardly be a star in such an unlikely situation.

It was certainly too glittering
and small for a glow-worm.
Who or what could it be?
Then, as he looked, it winked
at him, and so declared itself
to be an eye; and a small face
began gradually to grow up
round it, like a frame round a
picture. A brown little face,
with whiskers.

A grave round face, with the
same twinkle in its eye that
had first attracted his notice.

Small neat ears and thick
silky hair.

It was the Water Rat! Then the two animals stood and regarded each other cautiously.

"Hullo, Mole!" said the Water Rat.

"Hullo, Rat!" said the Mole.

"Would you like to come over?" inquired the Rat presently.

"Oh, it's all very well to talk," said the Mole, rather pettishly, he being new to a river and riverside life and its ways.

The Rat said nothing, but stooped and unfastened a rope and hauled on it; then lightly stepped into a little boat which the Mole had not observed. It was painted blue outside and white within, and was just the size for two animals; and the Mole's whole heart went out to it at once, even though he did not yet fully understand its uses.

The Rat sculled smartly across and made fast. Then he held up his fore-paw as the Mole stepped gingerly down. "Lean on that!" he said. "Now then, step lively!" and the Mole to his surprise and rapture found himself actually seated in the stern of a real boat.

"This has been a wonderful day!" said he, as the Rat shoved off and took to the sculls again. "Do you know, I've never been in a boat before in all my life."

"What?" cried the Rat, open-mouthed. "Never been in a — you never — well, I — what have you been doing, then?"

"Is it so nice as all that?" asked the Mole shyly, though he was quite prepared to believe it as he leant back in his seat and surveyed the cushions, the oars, the rowlocks, and all the fascinating fittings, and felt the boat sway lightly under him.

"Nice? It's the only thing," said the Water Rat solemnly, as he leant forward for his stroke. "Believe me, my young friend, there is nothing — absolutely nothing — half so much worth doing as simply messing about in boats. Simply messing," he went on dreamily, "messing—about—in—boats; messing—"

"Look ahead, Rat," cried the Mole suddenly, for looming perilously close was the bank.

It was too late. The boat struck
the bank full tilt and the Mole
gripped the sides anxiously.
The dreamer, the joyous oarsman,
lay on his back at the bottom
of the boat, his heels in the air.

"—about in boats — or with
boats," the Rat went on
composedly, picking himself up
with a pleasant laugh. "In or
out of 'em, it doesn't matter.
Nothing seems really to matter,
but that's the charm of it.
Whether you get away, or
whether you don't.

"Whether you arrive at your destination or whether you reach somewhere else, or whether you never get anywhere at all, you're always busy, and you never do anything in particular; and when you've done it there's always something else to do, and you can do it if you like, but you'd much better not. Look here! If you've really nothing else on hand this morning, supposing we drop down the river together, and have a long day of it?"

The Mole waggled his toes from sheer happiness, spread his chest with a sigh of full contentment, and leaned back blissfully into the soft cushions. "What a day I'm having!" he said. "Let us start at once!"

"Hold hard a minute, then!" said the Rat. He looped the painter through a ring in his landing-stage, climbed up into his hole above, and after a short interval reappeared staggering under a fat, wicker luncheon-basket.

"Shove that under your feet," he observed to the Mole, as he passed it down into the boat. Then he untied the painter and took the sculls again.

"What's inside it?" asked the Mole, wriggling with curiosity.

"There's cold chicken inside it," replied the Rat briefly, "coldtonguecoldhamcoldbeef pickledgherkinssaladfrenchrolls cresssandwhichespottedmeat gingerbeerlemonadesodawater—" "O stop, stop," cried the Mole in ecstasies: "This is too much!"

"Do you really think so?"
inquired the Rat seriously. "It's
only what I always take on these
little excursions; and the other
animals are always telling me
that I'm a mean beast and cut
it very fine!"

The Mole never heard a word he was saying. Absorbed in the new life he was entering upon, intoxicated with the sparkle, the ripple, the scents and the sounds and the sunlight, he trailed a paw in the water and dreamed long waking dreams. The Water Rat, like the good little fellow he was, sculled steadily on and forbore to disturb him.

"I like your clothes awfully, old chap," he remarked after some half an hour or so had passed.

"I'm going to get a black velvet smoking-suit myself some day, as soon as I can afford it."

"I beg your pardon," said the Mole, pulling himself together with an effort. "You must think me very rude; but all this is so new to me. So—this—is—a—River!"

"*The* River," corrected the Rat.

"And you really live by the river? What a jolly life!"

"By it and with it and on it and in it," said the Rat. "It's brother and sister to me, and aunts, and company, and food and drink, and (naturally) washing. It's my world, and I don't want any other. What it hasn't got is not worth having, and what it doesn't know is not worth knowing. Lord! the times we've had together! Whether in winter or summer, spring or autumn, it's always got its fun and its excitements. When the February floods come, and my cellars and basement are brimming, and the brown water runs by my best bedroom window."

"Or again when it all drops
away and shows patches of mud
that smells like plum-cake, and
the rushes and weed clog the
channels, and I can potter about
dry-shod over most of the bed
of it and find fresh food to eat,
and things careless people
have dropped out of boats!"

"But isn't it a bit dull at times?" the Mole ventured to ask. "Just you and the river, and no one else to pass a word with?"

"No one else to — well, I mustn't be hard on you," said the Rat with forbearance. "You're new to it, and of course you don't know. The bank is so crowded nowadays that many people are moving away altogether. O no, it isn't what it used to be, at all. Otters, kingfishers, dabchicks, moorhens, all of them about all day long and always wanting you to do something — as if a fellow had no business of his own to attend to!"

"What lies over there?" asked the Mole, waving a paw towards a background of woodland that darkly framed the water-meadows on one side of the river.

"That? O, that's just the Wild Wood," said the Rat shortly. "We don't go there very much, we river bankers."

"Aren't they — aren't they very nice people in there?" said the Mole a trifle nervously.

"W-e-ll," replied the Rat, "let me see. The squirrels are all right. And the rabbits — some of 'em, but rabbits are a mixed lot. And then there's Badger, of course. He lives right in the heart of it; wouldn't live anywhere else, either, if you paid him to do it. Dear old Badger! Nobody interferes with him. They'd better not," he added significantly.

"Why, who should interfere with him?" asked the Mole.

"Well, of course—there—are others," said the Rat slowly.

"Weasels—and stoats—and foxes—and so on. They're all right in a way—I'm very good friends with them —pass the time of day when we meet, and all that—but they break out sometimes, there's no denying it, and then — well, you can't really trust them, and that's the fact."

The Mole knew well that it is quite against animal-etiquette to dwell on possible trouble ahead, or even to allude to it; so he dropped the subject.

"And beyond the Wild Wood again?" he asked: "Where it's all blue and dim, and one sees what may be hills or perhaps they mayn't, and something like the smoke of towns, or is it only clouddrift."

"Beyond the Wild Wood comes the Wide World," said the Rat. "And that's something else."

"The Wide World doesn't matter, either to you or me. I've never been there, and I'm never going, nor you either, if you've got any sense at all. Don't ever refer to it again, please. Now then! Here's our backwater at last, where we're going to lunch."

Leaving the main stream, they now passed into what seemed at first sight like a little landlocked lake. Green turf sloped down to either edge, brown snaky tree-roots gleamed below the surface of the quiet water, while ahead of them the silvery shoulder and foamy tumble of a weir, arm-in-arm with a restless dripping mill-wheel, that held up in its turn a grey-gabled mill-house, filled the air with a soothing murmur of sound, dull and smothery, yet with little clear voices speaking up cheerfully out of it at intervals. It was so very beautiful that the Mole could only hold up both fore-paws and gasp, "O my! O my! O my!"

The Rat brought the boat
alongside the bank, made her
fast, helped the still awkward
Mole safely ashore, and swung
out the luncheon-basket. The
Mole begged as a favour to be
allowed to unpack it all by
himself; and the Rat was very
pleased to indulge him, and to
sprawl at full length on the grass
and rest, while his excited
friend shook out the table-cloth
and spread it on the ground,
then carefully took out all the
mysterious packets one by one.

Happily he arranged their contents in due order, still gasping, "O my! O my!" at each fresh revelation. When all was ready, the Rat said, "Now, pitch in, old fellow!" and the Mole was indeed very glad to obey, for he had started his spring-cleaning at a very early hour that morning, as people will do, and had not paused for bite or sup; and he had been through a very great deal since that distant time which now seemed so many days ago.

"What are you looking at?" said the Rat presently, when the edge of their hunger was somewhat dulled, and the Mole's eyes were able to wander off the tablecloth a little.

"I am looking," said the Mole, "at a streak of bubbles that I see travelling along the surface of the water. That is a thing that strikes me as funny."

"Bubbles? Oho!" said the Rat, and turning to the water, he chirruped cheerily in an inviting sort of way.

A broad glistening muzzle showed itself above the edge of the bank, and the Otter hauled himself out and shook the water from his coat.

"Greedy beggars!" he observed, making for the provender. "Why didn't you invite me, Ratty?"

"This was an impromptu affair," explained the Rat. "By the way — my friend, Mr Mole."

"Pleased to meet you."

"Proud, I'm sure," said the Otter, and the two animals were friends forthwith.

"Such a rumpus everywhere!" continued the Otter. "All the world seems out on the river to-day. I came up this backwater to try and get a moment's peace, and then stumbled upon you fellows! At least — I beg pardon — I don't exactly mean that, you know."

There was a rustle behind them, proceeding from a hedge wherein last year's leaves still clung thick, and a stripy head, with high shoulders behind it, peered forth on them.

"Come on, old Badger!" shouted the Rat.

The Badger trotted forward a pace or two; then grunted, "H'm! Company," and turning his back, he disappeared from view.

"That's just the sort of fellow he is," observed the disappointed Rat. "Simply hates Society! Now we shan't see any more of him today. Well, tell us who's out on the river?"

"Toad's out, for one," replied the Otter. "In his brand-new wager-boat; new togs, new everything!" The two animals looked at each other and laughed.

"Once, it was nothing but sailing," said the Rat. "Then he tired of that and took to punting. Nothing would please him but to punt all day and every day, and a nice mess he made of it.

Last year it was house-boating and we all had to go and stay with him in his houseboat, and pretend we liked it. He was going to spend the rest of his life in a house-boat.

"It's all the same; whatever he takes up, he gets tired of it, and starts on something fresh."

"Such a good fellow, too," remarked the Otter reflectively. "But no stability — especially in a boat!"

From where they sat they could get a glimpse of the main stream across the island that separated them; and just then a boat flashed into view, the rower — a short, stout figure — splashing badly and rolling a good deal, but working hard.

The Rat stood up and hailed him, but Toad — for it was he — shook his head and settled sternly to his work.

"He'll be out of the boat in a minute if he rolls like that," said the Rat, sitting down again.

"Of course he will," chuckled the Otter. "Did I ever tell you that good story about Toad and the lock-keeper? It happened this way. Toad..."

An errant May-fly swerved unsteadily athwart the current in the intoxicated fashion affected by young bloods of May-flies seeing like. A swirl of water and a "clop!" and the May-fly was visible no more.

Neither was the Otter. He had quite disappeared from view.

The Mole looked down. The voice was still in his ears, but the turf whereon he had sprawled was clearly vacant. Not an Otter to be seen, as far as the distant horizon.

But again there was a streak of bubbles on the surface of the river.

The rat hummed a tune, and the Mole recollected that animal-etiquette forbade any sort of comment on the sudden disappearance of one's friends at any moment, for any reason or no reason whatever, so, with great strength of will, he refrained from remarking on it.

"Well, well," said the Rat, "I suppose we ought to be moving. I wonder which of us had better pack the luncheon-basket?" He did not speak as if he was frightfully eager for the treat.

"O, please let me," said the Mole. So, of course, the Rat let him.

Packing the basket was not quite such pleasant work as unpacking the basket. Sadly, it never is.

But the Mole was bent on
enjoying everything, and
although just when he had got
the basket packed and strapped
up rightly he saw a plate staring
up at him from the grass, and,
when the job had been done
again, the Rat pointed out a
fork which anybody ought to
have seen, and last of all,
behold! the mustard-pot, which
he had been sitting on without
knowing it — still, somehow,
the thing got finished at last,
without much loss of temper.

The afternoon sun was getting low as the Rat sculled gently homewards in a dreamy mood, murmuring poetry-things over to himself, and not paying much attention to Mole. But the Mole was very full of lunch, and self-satisfaction, and pride, and already quite at home in a boat (so he thought) and was getting a bit restless besides; and presently he said, "Ratty! Please, I want to row, now!"

The Rat shook his head with a smile. "Not yet, my young friend," he said — "wait till you've had a few lessons. It's not so easy as it looks."

The Mole was quiet for a minute or two. But he began to feel more and more jealous of Rat, sculling so strongly and so easily along, and his pride began to whisper that he could do it every bit as well.

He jumped up and seized the sculls so suddenly that the Rat, who was gazing out over the water and saying more poetry-things to himself, was taken by surprise and fell backwards off his seat with his legs in the air for the second time, while the triumphant Mole took his place and grabbed the sculls with entire confidence.

"Stop it, you silly ass," cried the Rat, from the bottom of the boat. "You can't do it! You'll have us over."

The Mole refused to listen and flinging his sculls back with a flourish, he made a great dig at the water. He missed the surface altogether, his legs flew up above his head, and he found himself lying on the top of the prostrate Rat.

Greatly alarmed, the Mole
made a grab at the side of the
boat, and the next moment —
Sploosh!

Over went the boat, and he
found himself struggling in the
river.

O my, how cold the water was, and O, how very wet it felt. How it sang in his ears as he went down, down, down! How bright and welcome the sun looked as he rose to the surface coughing and spluttering! How black was his despair when he felt himself sinking again! Then a firm paw gripped him by the back of his neck. It was the Rat, and he was evidently laughing — the Mole could feel him shaking, right down his arm and through to his strong paw.

The Rat got hold of a scull and shoved it under the Mole's arm; then he did the same by the other side of him and, swimming behind, propelled the helpless animal to shore, hauled him out, and set him down on the bank, a squashy, pulpy lump of misery.

When the Rat had rubbed him down a bit, and wrung some of the wet out of him, he said, "Now then, old fellow! Trot up and down the towing-path as hard as you can, till you're warm and dry again, while I dive for the luncheon-basket."

So the dismal Mole, wet without and ashamed within, trotted about till he was fairly dry, while the Rat plunged into the water again, recovered the boat, righted her and made her fast, fetched his floating property to shore by degrees, including two plump cushions which were heading determinedly for the far bank, and finally dived successfully for the luncheon-basket and struggled to land it.

When all was ready for a start once more, the Mole, limp and dejected, took his seat in the stern of the boat; and as they set off, he said in a low voice, broken with emotion, "Ratty, my generous friend! I am very sorry for my foolish conduct.

"My heart quite fails me when
I think how I might have lost
that beautiful luncheon-basket.
Indeed, I have been a complete

ass, and I know it. Will you
overlook it this once and
forgive me, and let things go
on as before?"

"That's all right, bless you!"
responded the Rat cheerily.
"What's a little wet to a Water
Rat? I'm more in the water than
out of it most days. Don't you
think any more about it; and,
look here! I really think you had
better come and stop with me
for a little time. It's very plain
and rough, you know — not like
Toad's house at all — but you
haven't seen that yet; still, I
can make you comfortable. And
I'll teach you to row, and to swim,
and you'll soon be as handy on

the water as any of us."

The Mole was so touched by his kind manner of speaking that he could find no voice to answer him; and he had to brush away a tear or two with the back of his paw. But the Rat kindly looked in another direction, and presently the Mole's spirits revived again, and he was even able to give some straight back-talk to a couple of moorhens who were sniggering to each other about his bedraggled appearance.

When they got home, the Rat
made a bright fire in the parlour
and fetched down a dressing-
gown and slippers. Then he
planted the Mole in an arm-
chair in front of the blaze, and
told him river stories till
supper-time.

Very thrilling stories they were, too, to an earth-dwelling animal like Mole. Stories about weirs, and sudden floods, and leaping pike, and steamers that flung hard bottles — at least bottles were certainly flung, and from steamers, so presumably by them; and about herons, and how particular they were whom they spoke to; and about adventures down drains, and night-fishings with Otter, or excursions far afield with Badger. Supper was a most cheerful meal;

but very shortly afterwards a terribly sleepy Mole had to be escorted upstairs by his considerate host, to the best bedroom, where he soon laid his head on his pillow in great peace and contentment, knowing that his new-found friend the River was lapping the sill of his window.

This day was only the first of many similar ones for the emancipated Mole, each of them longer and fuller of interest as the ripening summer moved on.

He learnt to swim and to row, and entered into the joy of running water; and with his ear to the reedstems he caught, at intervals, something of what the wind went whispering so constantly among them.

but very shortly afterwards a terribly sleepy Mole had to be escorted upstairs by his considerate host, to the best bedroom, where he soon laid his head on his pillow in great peace and contentment, knowing that his new-found friend the River was lapping the sill of his window.

This day was only the first of many similar ones for the emancipated Mole, each of them longer and fuller of interest as the ripening summer moved on.

He learnt to swim and to row, and entered into the joy of running water; and with his ear to the reedstems he caught, at intervals, something of what the wind went whispering so constantly among them.

KENNETH GRAHAME

Kenneth Grahame (1859-1932) had always
longed to be a writer but he did not have the
support of his family, and instead began a
long career in the Bank of England.
He found time to write books and essays, but
none so well-known as *The Wind in the
Willows* which must endure as one of the
most enchanting stories ever written for
children. The author did in fact first tell it to
his own son, Alistair, who requested a
bedtime story about "moles, giraffes and
water rats". Kenneth Grahame continued the
tale in a series of letters sent to his son,
whom he nicknamed 'Mouse', and it was
later published in 1908.
The Riverbank is the first of four stories in
this new abridged version from Parragon
Mini Classics.